Penworthy 979.96 10-10

STOP SNORING, BERNARD!

ZACHARIAH OHORA

SQUARE
FISH

HENRY HOLT AND COMPANY
NEW YORK

With special thanks
to Robin Tordini

SQUARE
FISH

An Imprint of Macmillan

Library of Congress Cataloging-in-Publication Data
OHora, Zachariah.
Stop snoring, Bernard! / Zachariah OHora.
p.   cm.
Summary: Because his loud snores disturb all the other animals
at the zoo, Bernard the otter tries to find a solution.
ISBN 978-1-250-00717-9
[1. Otters—Fiction. 2. Snoring—Fiction. 3. Zoo animals—Fiction.
4. Zoos—Fiction.] I. Title.
PZ7.O41405St 2010   [E]—dc22   2009005265

Originally published in the United States by Henry Holt and Company
First Square Fish Edition: February 2012
Square Fish logo designed by Filomena Tuosto
Book designed by Véronique Lefèvre Sweet
mackids.com

10 9 8 7 6 5 4 3 2 1

AR: 1.6

THE ZOO

To Lydia, my love

Bernard loved living at the zoo.
He loved mealtime, playtime,
and best of all . . .

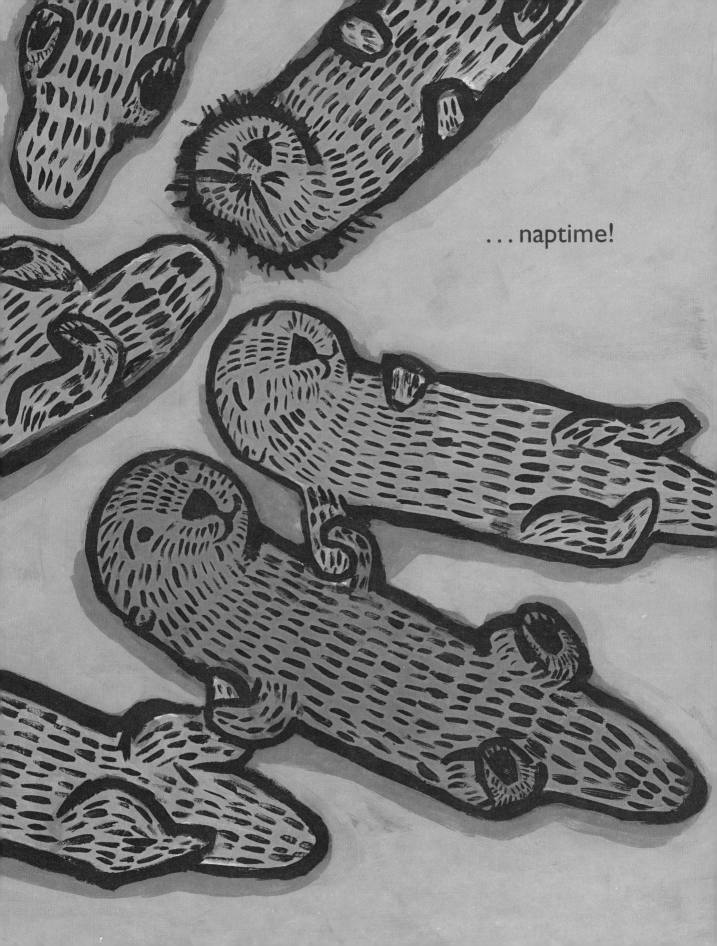

. . . naptime!

But there was one little problem.
Bernard snored . . . LOUDLY!

One afternoon at naptime,
Grumpy Giles had had enough.
"Snore somewhere else,
Bernard!" he said.

Bernard tried sleeping in a lake, but that didn't work.

He tried sleeping in a fountain,
but that didn't work either.

SN

He even tried sleeping in a puddle!
But that *really* didn't work.

Bernard was sad
and lonely.
He found a tucked-
away place, curled up
by himself, and drifted
off to sleep.

The other otters missed Bernard.
They searched for him all through
the night.

BERNARD!

The next morning Bernard woke up and
saw hundreds of bats on the ceiling.

"Excuse me!" he said. "How did you
sleep with all my snoring?"

"We didn't," replied a bat. "We were out
all night and now we are trying to sleep. So
please don't snore here."

Bernard felt terrible. There wasn't anyplace
he could sleep without bothering somebody.
He trudged toward the zoo gate.
But then he heard something.

It was the other otters!

"We couldn't sleep without you," said
Grumpy Giles. "And I'm sorry I yelled.
Please come back."

And from that day on, everyone
napped happily. Well, almost everyone.